Samuel French Acting Edition

I0591771

Dreams of Flying
Dreams of Falling

by Adam Rapp

SAMUELFRENCH.COM   SAMUELFRENCH.CO.UK

FOR PRODUCTION ENQUIRIES

UNITED STATES AND CANADA
Info@SamuelFrench.com
1-866-598-8449

UNITED KINGDOM AND EUROPE
Plays@SamuelFrench.co.uk
020-7255-4302

Each title is subject to availability from Samuel French, depending
upon country of performance. Please be aware that DREAMS OF
FLYING DREAMS OF FALLING may not be licensed by Samuel
French in your territory. Professional and amateur producers should
contact the nearest Samuel French office or licensing partner to verify
availability.

MUSIC USE NOTE

Licensees are solely responsible for obtaining formal written permission from copyright owners to use copyrighted music in the performance of this play and are strongly cautioned to do so. If no such permission is obtained by the licensee, then the licensee must use only original music that the licensee owns and controls. Licensees are solely responsible and liable for all music clearances and shall indemnify the copyright owners of the play(s) and their licensing agent, Samuel French, against any costs, expenses, losses and liabilities arising from the use of music by licensees. Please contact the appropriate music licensing authority in your territory for the rights to any incidental music.

IMPORTANT BILLING AND CREDIT REQUIREMENTS

If you have obtained performance rights to this title, please refer to your licensing agreement for important billing and credit requirements.

DREAMS OF FLYING DREAMS OF FALLING, presented by the Atlantic Theater Company, premiered at Classic Stage Company in New York City on October 3, 2011. The performance was directed by Neil Pepe, with sets by Andrew Boyce and Takeshi Kata, costumes by Theresa Squire, lighting by Tyler Micoleau, and music and sound by David Van Tieghem. The cast was as follows:

SANDRA	Christine Lahti
WILMA	Quincy Tyler Bernstine
DIRK	Cotter Smith
BERT	Reed Birney
CORA	Katherine Waterston
CELESTE	Betsy Aidem
JAMES	Shane McRae

CHARACTERS

SANDRA

WILMA

DIRK

BERT

CORA

CELESTE

JAMES

(The dining room of a wealthy American home belonging to the Cabots. A chandelier looming over an impressive, impeccably dressed dinner table. High-end, ornate table settings. An intercom housed in the wall near the entrance to the kitchen. A bay window looking out onto a pond, a gazebo, and an ancient willow tree. The light in the window should suggest early evening. An entrance to the kitchen. An entrance to the living room. Another entrance downstage left, which leads to the basement.)

*(**SANDRA CABOT** [pronounced "Saundra"] – white, older-middle-aged, very fit, sexy, cutthroat – enters with a floral arrangement in a vase. She wears high-end Chanel, a Rolex, fine shoes. She sets the floral arrangement on the table, primps it a bit.)*

*(**WILMA**, an African-American woman of thirty, enters next with a carafe of decanted wine. She wears a tasteful uniform, but nothing suggesting the maidservant that she has been hired to be. She sets the wine on the sideboard.)*

SANDRA. Merci, Wilma.

WILMA. Que fleurs belles.

SANDRA. Quelles belles *fleurs*, Wilma. Quelles belles *fleurs*.

WILMA. Quelles belles fleurs.

*(**WILMA** crosses to the table, takes over primping the flowers. **SANDRA** gently corrects **WILMA**'s primping. **WILMA** makes the proper adjustment.)*

(From offstage, the sounds of men talking, joking. **WILMA** *exits.)*

(Sandra's husband, **DR. BERTRAM CABOT**, *enters. He is white, balding with wisps of hair. He wears a loose linen suit, a bow tie, and white bucks. He has a paunch. His arm is around his old friend* **DIRK VON STOFENBERG**, *a vigorous fifty-ish dealmaker wearing Nantucket Reds, a summer blazer, a club tie, and topsiders. He is fit and handsome, possesses a thick head of hair, looks younger than his age. The men are laughing, carrying highball glasses of scotch.)*

DIRK. A monkey?! A *monkey*, are you kidding me?!

BERT. A Borneon orangutan.

DIRK. Borneo – that's Africa, right?

SANDRA. Southeast Asia.

BERT. Borneo is actually part of Malaysia, Dirk.

SANDRA. It's the third-largest island in the world.

BERT. Sandra and I spent our honeymoon there.

DIRK. I thought you guys went to Bangladesh.

SANDRA. Bangladesh is where Tippy and Bunny Saltonstall went to photograph the rice fields.

DIRK. The rice fields! Those photographs were wonderful!

BERT. Those poor oppressed workers.

SANDRA. I found the collection to be sentimental and condescendingly sophomoric. And if I remember correctly it's where Tippy contracted a wicked case of dysentery that followed him back to the states.

DIRK. That's right, he lost all that weight. Everyone thought he was dying.

SANDRA. We never travel without the Cipro, do we Bertram?

BERT. We don't leave the country without it.

SANDRA. The *country*. I don't leave *Connecticut*. You can't even trust the tap water at restaurants anymore and that's the god's honest.

(She crosses to the intercom, presses a button.)

(Into intercom.) Wilma, be a dear and pour me a few fingers of Laphroaig in a highball glass, please?

(To **DIRK**.*)* And just for the record, Dirk, Bangladesh is technically in *South* Asia.

BERT. It's actually not all that far from Borneo.

SANDRA. If you happen to be in a spaceship staring down at the *continent*.

DIRK. Hey, I heard you can do that now! With a little bit of training, they'll take you up into space and let you take in the sights! It costs an arm and a leg but what an experience! Could you imagine that? Walking on the Moon or some such? Talking on your cell phone? Taking a galactic stroll?

(Awkward pause.)

BERT. Anyway, Dirk, Borneo was just fantastic. You remember this. Sandra and I stayed in that bamboo hut with a roof made of elephant ears and bat guano. It overlooked the Sulu Sea.

SANDRA. The whole place smelled of pickled prawns and sewage and the mosquitoes were unbearable.

BERT. But at night the jungle was absolutely symphonic. The music of baboons and tropical birds. Insects the size of small cats. A place where nature and mythology seemed inseparable.

DIRK. It sounds wonderful.

BERT. And the caves, my god, the caves! Stalactites and stalagmites all around you. Like walking through the jaws of some Orwellian monster. And these pockets of profound darkness. You got the feeling you could lose yourself in those caves. Like really lose yourself.

SANDRA. Speaking of losing things, Captain Chromdome over here lost our passports in the Rajang River.

DIRK. Oh, no!

SANDRA. Oh, *yes*. We became instantly vulnerable. The locals could smell it like a disease. We literally must have put off an odor.

BERT. I've never been entirely sure about that interpretation, honey.

SANDRA. Bertram, they were on us like flies on shit. Their gaping mouths and hollow, sunken eyes. Soft, half-grown teeth like niblits of corn. The wretched sound of their whining voices. They practically surrounded us, Dirk. It was as though they wanted to cook us in a stew.

DIRK. What did you do?

SANDRA. I screamed, "BACK OFF, INDIGENOUS PEOPLES OF BORNEO! BACK OFF WITH YOUR SMALL UNDERDEVELOPED HANDS AND SWOLLEN STOMACHS!! BACK THE FUCK OFF!!"

DIRK. And did they?

SANDRA. They retreated like goats on a hillock.

BERT. All you have to do is raise your voice.

SANDRA. It worked in Borneo and it certainly worked in Thailand when we had to return that awful soup that smelled of some old lady's incontinence.

BERT. It works in most European countries, too.

SANDRA. But you have to scream "fuck" and you have to *mean* it.

> (**WILMA** *enters with a highball of scotch, hands it to* **SANDRA**.)

DIRK. Fuck. I mean fudge. I mean fun.

SANDRA. Merci, Wilma.

WILMA. Bon appétit, Madame.

> (**WILMA** *exits.*)

DIRK. Is she French?

SANDRA. No, but she's learning.

BERT. It's kind of like our own little continuing ed program. Berlitz French, state capitals, Shakespearean sonnets.

SANDRA. We pay her handsomely, put her up in the guest house, and she gets an education to boot.

DIRK. Is she from the city?

SANDRA. Red Hook, Brooklyn. Caitlin Aranduff hired her twin sister and she and Ashton have been quite pleased. As have we.

BERT. Cora's just crazy about her.

SANDRA. Cora's crazy about anyone who wasn't raised wearing Nantucket Reds and topsiders. Nothing like having an overly educated lefty daughter who's never *left* the house.

> (**DIRK** *realizes that he is wearing Nantucket Reds and topsiders.*)

DIRK. Should I buzz home and change my clothes?

SANDRA. Don't you dare change a thing, you're fantastic!

> (*Beat.*)

DIRK. Cora's probably just going through a phase.

SANDRA. Four years is not a phase, Dirk, it's practically an epoch. She's twenty-six years old for godsakes.

DIRK. But she graduated from Harvard. And with honors if I remember correctly. That's no small feat.

SANDRA. Yes, don't remind me. The girl has a Harvard degree and she's never worked a day in her life. She has no ambition – none that I know of anyway.

BERT. She has her art project.

SANDRA. What art project? Have you seen a single piece of evidence that she's creating art up there? She's creating art and I'm creating a Martian language. And it's not as if she's agoraphobic or somehow mentally incapable. She's just spoiled and bored and undersexed. She's a beautiful girl, and in addition to working she should be out there ruining men.

> (*Awkward pause.*)

DIRK. So what wound up happening in Borneo, did you get new passports?

SANDRA. Yes. I practically had to blow the official at the American consulate.

BERT. I left the room of course.

SANDRA. For the past thirty-five years, Bertram has developed a special talent for leaving rooms at moments that hurtle precipitously toward, shall we say, inevitability.

(Awkward pause.)

BERT. So, back to that orangutan.

DIRK. Yeah. Hey, by the way, are orangutans monkeys or apes?

BERT. I believe they're apes.

SANDRA. They're actually *great* apes.

BERT. Anyway, at this place in Ojai, California – at this ex-internet mogul's vast compound – this highly domesticated primate – this orangutan that could perform perfect sign language and paint watercolors and operate kitchen appliances and drive golf carts, this veritable simian *genius*, completely snapped and pulled his master's appendages off.

DIRK. Appendages?! What appendages?! What does that *mean*?!

BERT. Well, it pulled off his left arm...and his right hand... and his genitals.

SANDRA. For godsakes, just say COCK, Bertram! COCK!

BERT. Okay, okay, it pulled off his cock. I mean, can you even imagine that? Signing hello to your loyal, civilized pet and *pop*, there goes your hand, *pop*, there goes your arm –

DIRK. Pop, there goes Yankee Doodle Dandy! Then what happened?

BERT. Well, he died. Arterial lagoons at the ape house. The poor man's wife eventually happens upon the mess, calls for help. Apparently, when the authorities arrive, the orangutan's wearing his master's clothes. It had stripped him naked and defecated on his ravaged body. Placed the detached hand over his heart. The genitals on his forehead. The arm where his genitals were. I mean, what *is* that, an attempt at irony? Some sort of corporeal jigsaw joke? Species jealousy? The authorities killed the orangutan on-site, of course. It's just a crazy story.

DIRK. Jesus.

SANDRA. Jesus was at best a Nazarean folk singer with high metabolism, a velveteen deejay voice, and pleasant, dilated pupils. Don't get me started on Jesus.

(*Beat.*)

DIRK. I had no idea monkeys could be so savage.

SANDRA. Apes, Dirk. Monkeys dress up in bellboy uniforms and play the drums.

DIRK. I mean apes.

BERT. From the Primate Superfamily Hominoidea. We're apes, too.

SANDRA. Dirk, you're looking exceedingly well, by the way. Don't you think so, Bertram?

BERT. Dirk's always been very impressive.

SANDRA. *Impressive?* This goes far beyond some bland, indistinguishable adjective reserved for automotive innovation. It's what he contributes to the *species*. He's handsome and virile and charming.

DIRK. Tell my wife! I could use the PR!

SANDRA. Where is Celeste, anyway?

DIRK. She should be here any minute. Since James has been home it's not been easy coaxing him out of the house.

SANDRA. Well, it's only been a few days, right?

DIRK. Almost a week, actually.

BERT. Two years is a long time.

DIRK. Stockbridge was a very good thing. We missed him but it took that long for him to get his bearings, it really did... By the way, thanks for tonight. It's so nice of you to invite us over. I know it just means the world to Celeste. And to James, too, of course.

SANDRA. We've all missed him, Dirk. And we're so glad that he's well again. What happened to your son was just tragic. Tragic for us all. And we're so thrilled that he's back.

BERT. It's the least we could do. I know Cora is looking forward to seeing him.

SANDRA. Talk about not leaving the house. She has no excuse. *(Pressing a button on the intercom.)* Cora, darling, could you come down here, please? Our guests are arriving.

(Awkward pause.)

DIRK. Sandra, Bert was just telling me that you guys might be going to Costa Rica for your thirtieth.

SANDRA. That is the plan.

DIRK. I hear it's beautiful there. Just tremendous flora and fauna.

SANDRA. So long as we steer clear of those savage primates.

BERT. I was just showing him the brochures.

DIRK. I've never seen such wonderful brochures! The colors!

BERT. The one with the toucan on the front. The toucan in the rainforest, looking grave and senatorial.

SANDRA. Bertram, next time you use the loo, make sure to trim your nostril hair.

*(**BERT** touches his nose self-consciously.)*

What is flora and fauna, anyway? I've never actually known what that means.

DIRK. I think it might be plants. Plants and animals and such. Kind of all mixed up together... Or a shimmering waterfall. Or like a rock with a bird on it. Is that right, Bert?

SANDRA. Dirk, I must say, you are looking conspicuously fit.

DIRK. Thank you, Sandra.

SANDRA. I've always been so impressed with your physique. Bertram, haven't we always been so impressed with Dirk's physique?

BERT. Men our age should be so lucky.

SANDRA. You stand like a field general. You take stairs two at a time. I've never seen you struggle to disembark from a chair. Have you ever seen Dirk here struggle while disembarking from a chair, Bertram?

BERT. I can't say that I have.

SANDRA. Do you ever have lower back pain?

DIRK. No.

SANDRA. Arthritis?

DIRK. Nope.

SANDRA. I imagine you bend at the waist easily, am I right?

DIRK. I mean, I can still touch my toes without much of a hassle.

SANDRA. Yes you can, can't you... I look at you and I think you could have been a light-heavyweight boxer. Or a lugist.

DIRK. The luge! I love the luge! That's those guys on the sleds, right?

SANDRA. May I poke you?

DIRK. Poke me?

SANDRA. Yes, a harmless prod to your midsection. I'd like that very much. May I?

DIRK. Um... Bert?

BERT. Hello. I mean, I don't mind.

DIRK. Okay, then. Poke away!

　　　　(**SANDRA** *pokes* **DIRK** *in the tummy.*)

SANDRA. You're trim, Dirk. Poke him, Bertram.

BERT. Now, honey.

SANDRA. Go on.

BERT. But Dirk doesn't want that.

SANDRA. Why don't you ask him?

BERT. Do you want me to do that, Dirk? Do you want me to poke you?

DIRK. Uh, sure. Bert. Why not!

　　　　(**BERT** *pokes him.*)

SANDRA. You feel that?

　　　(To **DIRK.***)* How have you managed to keep so firm all these years?

DIRK. To tell you the truth, I don't know. Must be –

SANDRA. The brisk walks to the shore?

DIRK. Well, I used to walk to the train station every morning –

SANDRA. The pre-dawn cross-training regiment? Tell him what we know about Fitness Corps dot com, Bertram.

BERT. It's a fitness website. It posts the workout of the day. You can download instructional videos.

SANDRA. Imagine three Amazonian women power squatting with fifty-pound barbells thrust mightily over their heads. Thighs like sculpted marble. Do you take glucosamine, Dirk?

DIRK. No, I don't.

SANDRA. Vitamin B-12? Omega fish oil tablets?

DIRK. I don't take anything.

SANDRA. Well, what's your secret? How do you stay such an Adonis?

DIRK. Um, I drink apple juice.

SANDRA. Have you ever studied tai chi or zen budokai jujitsu?

DIRK. No.

SANDRA. You've attempted that, haven't you, Bertram?

BERT. I tried that, yes.

SANDRA. Tell me it's isometric.

DIRK. Um –

SANDRA. Plyometric.

DIRK. I have no idea –

SANDRA. Or your vigorous colonics program and master cleanses.

DIRK. Master *who*?

SANDRA. Tell him about the Master Cleanse, Bertram.

BERT. Lemon juice, cayenne, and grade-B maple syrup. Ten days works absolute wonders.

SANDRA. Well, for some people it does. For you it just made you more flatulent and ashamed of the concept of your own anus.

(Something thuds against the bay window.)

DIRK. What was that?!

SANDRA. *(Looking out the window.)* Goddamn birds.

BERT. We're having a bit of a Canadian Geese problem.

DIRK. We get them too. Celeste enjoys feeding them bread crusts and the like.

BERT. Unfortunately they've been meddling in our garden.

SANDRA. They meddle in the garden and shit all over the gazebo. Not to mention the awful honking. Goddamn parasites.

> *(She crosses to the intercom, presses a button.)*

(Into intercom.) Wilma, will you come in here, please?

> **(WILMA** *enters.)*

Did we find a solution for the geese?

WILMA. Yes, ma'am. Should be here tomorrow.

SANDRA. Wilma, this is our longtime friend, Dirk Von Stofenberg.

DIRK. *(Offering his hand.)* Nice to meet you, Wilma.

WILMA. Nice to meet you.

> *(They shake chastely.)*

DIRK. Your French sounds terrific, by the way.

WILMA. Thanks.

SANDRA. *(Gently correcting her.)* Merci.

WILMA. *(To* **DIRK.***)* Merci.

DIRK. You're quite welcome.

SANDRA. *(To* **WILMA.***)* You may go.

> **(WILMA** *exits.)*

BERT. What's the solution for the geese?

SANDRA. Special food pellets. That they will ingest. And be dispatched.

BERT. Can we *do* that?

SANDRA. Of course we can do that, it's from France. You can do pretty much anything if it's from France, right, Dirk?

DIRK. If you say so, Sandra!

SANDRA. I do say so. Oui, oui, mon cheval magnifique. And I'd also like to say that you have fantastic hair. May I tell you that?

DIRK. You're talking about my hair?

SANDRA. Yes, that silvery mass of fine flexible protein strands that grows from follicles on the crown of your head. May I compliment you on your dazzling hair?

DIRK. Bert, help me out here.

BERT. It's fine with me, pal, it really is.

SANDRA. May I run my hands through it?

DIRK. Um, sure.

> (**SANDRA** *moves close to him, runs her hands through his hair.*)

SANDRA. You don't seem to be losing any.

DIRK. Lucky genes, I guess.

SANDRA. Lucky indeed.

> (*She is transfixed by his hair.*)

BERT. I think I'll...

> (*He exits.* **SANDRA** *and* **DIRK** *are left alone.* **SANDRA** *crosses to the intercom, presses a button.*)

SANDRA. (*Into intercom.*) Wilma, the dining room is smelling a bit *éventé*, would you mind coming in here and cracking a window?

> (**WILMA** *enters, cracks a window.*)

And will you take care of the bird please?

WILMA. Oui, Madame.

> (*She begins to exit.*)

SANDRA. (*To* **WILMA.**) Oh, and one more thing?

> (**WILMA** *stops.*)

WILMA. Oui, Madame?

SANDRA. What's the state capital of Connecticut?

WILMA. I believe it's Hartford.

SANDRA. I have no idea why our nation's founders chose one of the many armpits of our state as its capital but you are correct. Well done.

WILMA. Merci.

(She exits. After a pause:)

SANDRA. I had a dream about you, Dirk.

DIRK. You did?

SANDRA. I did indeed. Would you like to know the details?

DIRK. Um –

SANDRA. We were riding bareback on a horse. A lathery thunderhorse. Black as polished onyx. Save for matching larrigan boots, we were naked and the sun was making us sweat into each other and you had an enormous uncircumcised penis that gleamed like a scepter. We galloped through woodlands and rolling hillsides. Beasts of all persuasions watched us hungrily. Jealous birds circled overhead. Hawks and eagles and peregrine falcons halted mid-flight to behold our revelation of nature. We rode out to the shore of an ink-green sea where we made love in the boiling froth. You were so deep inside me I could feel you in my throat. When I woke up my underwear was drenched. My bed smelled of coconut and papaya. I haven't felt that sensation in a very long time, Dirk. A very very long time. Do you find me attractive?

DIRK. I've always thought you were a beautiful woman, Sandra. Bert's a lucky man.

SANDRA. Have you ever dreamed about me?

DIRK. No. But I've only ever had one dream. When I was twelve.

SANDRA. What was it about?

DIRK. I dreamed that I could fly. It was night and the stars were huge. When I passed through the Milky Way there was music. Trombones mostly. Like Fourth of July parade music. I could see the sun silvering the horizon. I breathed in a star. I've never felt so free. It seemed like the dream would go on forever… But when I passed over Hawaii I fell thousands of feet into a volcano and died. When I woke up my arms were numb and I had wet the bed. What are larrigan boots?

SANDRA. A larrigan is a knee-high boot with the leg part made of oiled leather, worn especially by lumberjacks, trappers, and woodsmen.

DIRK. You certainly have an impressive vocabulary.

SANDRA. And you certainly possess untold impressive gifts. Have you ever fantasized about making love to me?

DIRK. Sandra...

SANDRA. I'll ask you again, Dirk. Have you ever fantasized about making love to me, yes or no?

DIRK. I believe I have, yes.

SANDRA. In what positions? Missionary? Doggy style? Tractor trailer? The two-headed hobgoblin?

DIRK. Doggy style. And missionary. And standing...with your back against my General Electric Side-by-Side Refrigerator.

SANDRA. That model is enormous, is it not?

DIRK. It's rather large, yes.

SANDRA. Like you, I gather. What am I wearing?

DIRK. You mean right now or in my fantasy?

SANDRA. In your fantasy.

DIRK. You're wearing almost exactly what you're wearing right now except you don't have any pants on.

SANDRA. How wonderfully naughty. Answer me something, Dirk, are you circumsized?

DIRK. No.

SANDRA. You see? Somehow I knew that.

(*Beat.*)

Dirk, I'd like you to help me kill my husband.

DIRK. What? Why?

SANDRA. Because I can't take it anymore. He's killing me.

DIRK. I don't understand.

SANDRA. He's withering, Dirk. He's no longer a man. He's not even a woman. He's a slug with nipples. A Nerf ball with a mouth.

DIRK. But I don't find him effeminate at all.

SANDRA. It's worse than male femininity. It's a spineless, feeble, kindhearted powerlessness! It's practically Christian and it disgusts me! I simply refuse to spend the rest of my life continuing to enact this ridiculous marital husbandry. It's as if someone has played a cruel joke and swapped the Bertram I fell in love with with this embarrassing puppet version.

DIRK. Is he ill or something?

SANDRA. If by ill you mean does he have asphyxiating halitosis, the toes of a clubfooted warlock, and acute difficulty achieving and maintaining an erection, then he is *diseased*.

DIRK. Why not just divorce him? It would be the civilized thing to do.

SANDRA. Dirk, the divorce would drag on for years. Years I simply don't want to lose.

DIRK. There are rules, Sandra.

SANDRA. Surely you don't live by strict modes of morality now, do you? I don't buy that for a minute. Of all people, you should appreciate the finer shades of gray. Of all people, Dirk.

DIRK. Bert's one of my oldest friends, Sandra. We've known each other since Yale.

SANDRA. Yale was thirty-five years ago.

DIRK. We rowed crew together. We won the Regatta.

SANDRA. You did indeed win the Regatta. You finally beat Harvard after a three-year drought and you were the captain. As a sophomore. Crew captain as a sophomore. Remarkable.

DIRK. And Bert was a big part of that.

SANDRA. Bertram was the coxswain. *[Pronounced "coxen."]*

DIRK. But the coxswain is arguably the most important member of the team. He's Master of the Vessel.

SANDRA. Oh, come on Dirk, the coxswain is basically a male cheerleader. He might as well be wearing pigtails and a skirt.

DIRK. Bert was the toast of New Haven. We wouldn't have won the Regatta without him.

SANDRA. *You* were the toast of New Haven, Dirk. Bertram was the crouton. In fact he was a lightly *toasted* crouton and he should have been relegated to the undergraduate salad bar.

DIRK. But you fell in love with that crouton. If I remember correctly, that's precisely the time when you two met. You came down from Northampton with Swifty Linderhoff and those lesbians from Miss Porter's.

SANDRA. Do you remember the fight song?

DIRK. Of course I remember the fight song.

SANDRA. What is it?

DIRK. *(Saying it, not singing.)* Bulldog Bulldog/Bow, wow, wow/Eli Yale/Bulldog Bulldog/Bow, wow, wow/ Our team can never fail/When the sons of Eli/Break through the line/This is the sign we hail/Bulldog Bulldog/Bow, wow, wow/Eli Yale...

SANDRA. Bertram doesn't remember it.

DIRK. Sure he does.

SANDRA. Dirk, Bertram Cornelius Cabot wouldn't know the fight song if an unneutered Bulldog in a navy blue turtleneck walked up to him and bit him in the ass. Those years mean nothing to him.

　　　　(Beat.)

How are things at home?

DIRK. Things at home are fine.

SANDRA. Are they really?

DIRK. Well, they have been a bit strained since James –

SANDRA. Dirk, James has only been home for six days. They've been strained for a lot longer than that.

(**DIRK** *says nothing.*)

Are you and Celeste still having sex?

DIRK. Sandra...

SANDRA. Do you still love her?

DIRK. Of course I love her.

SANDRA. But are you *in* love with her? Really be honest with yourself.

(**DIRK** *says nothing.*)

Let's just forget the rules for one night, Dirk. For one simple night. Think about what we could have.

DIRK. We?

SANDRA. Yes, We. Why not?

DIRK. Where would we go?

SANDRA. Anywhere we'd choose to. Monaco, Copenhagen, Bordeaux. Anywhere in the world. Have you ever swum in the reefs of the Red Sea? Or watched the sun rise in Mozambique?

DIRK. I can't say that I have?

SANDRA. It's liable to take your breath away, Dirk. The colors along the horizon. Violets. Burnt oranges. Colors that haven't even been invented yet. And no one would know we were there. Not a soul would know us for thousands of miles. We could take an apartment in Maputo. Or disappear in the Lebombo Mountains... Clean slate, Dirk. Or say No right now and I'll forget I ever mentioned any of this.

DIRK. And then what?

SANDRA. And then Celeste and James will arrive. And we'll finish our cocktails and move on to dinner and dessert and a fine aperitif. And we'll smile and laugh and take turns telling wonderful stories and the evening will turn into a pleasant anecdote that you and your wife and son can politely recount to each other on the car ride home.

And then later on, much later, deep in the middle of the night, while lying in bed with sweet Celeste, while staring up at the ceiling and listening to the central air turn itself on and off, you can continue to entomb yourself in that awful, unbearable, refrigerated silence and wonder what the next season of your life might have been... All you have to say is No.

(**DIRK** *opens his mouth. Closes his mouth.*)

So here's what will happen: When I say, "The grenadine came from the finest Himalayan pomegranates" you simply need to pour this liquid in Bertram's after-dinner digestif.

(*She sets the vial on the table.*)

It's an untraceable substance. "The grenadine came from the finest Himalayan pomegranates."

DIRK. How do you know it's untraceable?

SANDRA. Because I paid twenty-five thousand dollars for it.

DIRK. What exactly will happen to him?

SANDRA. Within minutes of ingesting it he'll grow very tired. And he'll simply want to lie down and fall asleep. And he'll painlessly float away. As if he's in a boyhood canoe.

(*She moves to the intercom.*)

(*Into intercom.*) Wilma, can you please bring out the grenadine?

(**DIRK** *starts to say something.*)

Dirk, sometimes life gives us the opportunity to do something extraordinary.

(**WILMA** *enters with a bottle of the finest grenadine in the world, sets it on the sideboard.* **DIRK** *palms the vial.*)

Thank you, Wilma. You may return to the kitchen. À tout à l'heure.

WILMA. À tout à l'heure.

(**WILMA** *exits.*)

SANDRA. Here, let me freshen your drink.

(She takes **DIRK**'s *highball glass, exits.* **DIRK** *is stunned, confused.)*

(Moments later, **CORA CABOT** *enters from downstage left. She is twenty-six, tall, oddly beautiful. She wears a simple, knee-length black shift. Tied around her waist is a velvet pouch. She is barefoot. Her hair is dark, as are her eyes. She wears no makeup save for a bit of black eyeliner, and is in general a bit ghostly. She eases into the room.)*

DIRK. Hello, Cora.

CORA. I can see you.

DIRK. I can see you, too.

CORA. Not the way I can see you.

DIRK. Well, what exactly do you see?

CORA. Someone who's never really been a full person.

DIRK. A full person.

CORA. Yes, a person who's not all there.

DIRK. Well, where else am I?

CORA. You might want to check the backyard. Under the weeping willow. You might run into him there later.

(Beat. **CORA** *starts to exit upstage toward the living room.)*

DIRK. You're not wearing any shoes.

CORA. Sometimes I don't wear anything at all. I can go on for days that way.

DIRK. Huh.

CORA. May I have a sample of your arm hair?

DIRK. My arm hair?

CORA. The hair on your arm, yes. I just need a little.

DIRK. What for?

CORA. My art project. Roll up your sleeve.

*(***DIRK** *rolls up his sleeve.* **CORA** *approaches him, feels his forearm for a moment, pinches*

*some arm hair between her fingers, and
yanks it out.* **DIRK** *winces, perhaps even jerks
a bit, but makes very little sound.* **CORA**
*removes the small pouch from around her
waist, undoes the top, places the arm hair
in it, closes the pouch, and returns it to her
waist.)*

CORA. You've had quite the lucky streak lately, wouldn't
you agree?

DIRK. I really don't know what you're referring to, Cora.

CORA. All that business with everyone losing their money.
The king of the jungle got caught, but somehow all the
other animals got away, scot-free.

DIRK. What exactly are you suggesting?

CORA. I'm not suggesting anything, Mr. Von Stofenberg.
I'm simply talking about luck. Some people have it and
some people don't. It's like hazel eyes or leaping ability.
I'm feeling lucky right now, just being near you.
(Looking at her arm.) I can practically feel my pores
dilating. Do you see that? How my skin's going all
prickly? ...Don't you think it's interesting how certain
animals are allowed to run wild through the jungle?
No matter how scary things get? I saw this film about
migrating wildebeests. The whole herd has to cross a
river in the Sudan. The river is teeming with crocodiles.
A congregation of crocodiles, waiting in the water.
Silent as cinnamon. Only ten percent of the wildebeests
make it. The others get torn limb from limb. I'll never
forget those crocodiles. Their ruthless pursuit. Their
surprising quickness and power. Almost surgical in
their collective precision. The snapping of their smiling
jaws. And the screaming wildebeests. It's a sound I've
never heard before. Almost human in its desperation.
Like a woman whose throat is about to be cut... Only
ten percent of those wildebeests made it to the other
side of that river. You're one of the lucky ones, Mr. Von
Stofenberg. And now everything's all funny with the
money. All the money's funny and the sunny days aren't

so sunny. And all those wonderful foundations had to close. Like the one that helped the leukemia babies... The randomness of luck.

(Holding her arm up.) Look at my arm. Do you see that?

(Awkward pause.)

DIRK. *(A desperate change of subject.)* I understand you're looking forward to seeing James.

CORA. When you look at him do you see yourself?

DIRK. Of course I do. I'm his father.

CORA. How do you think you're most alike?

(DIRK thinks for a moment.)

DIRK. Our hands. We have the same hands.

(CORA takes one of his hands in hers, inspects it, the front, the back.)

CORA. Can you keep a secret?

DIRK. Sure.

CORA. Swear on your life.

DIRK. ...Okay.

CORA. Say it.

DIRK. I swear on my life.

CORA. There's a lion in the basement.

DIRK. Really?

CORA. A she-lion from Africa.

DIRK. In the basement?

CORA. The subterranean story directly below us, yes. You know what a she-lion is, right?

DIRK. Of course.

CORA. She's not well.

DIRK. You're a very interesting girl, Cora.

(CORA releases his hand, exits.)

(DIRK realizes that he is still holding the vial in his other hand, puts it in his pocket. He crosses to the window, peers out at the sky,

*lifts his hand, touches the glass where the
goose had hit, lowers his hand. He then crosses
to the intercom, presses a button. The sound
of a lion issues forth. Not a full-fledged roar,
but definitely a lion. He releases the button.)*

(WILMA enters.)

WILMA. Did you need something, Sir?

DIRK. No, I... No, Wilma. I'm fine, thanks.

(WILMA exits.)

*(DIRK moves to touch the intercom again.
Just as he is about to press a button, SANDRA
enters with drinks, hands his to him.)*

SANDRA. Your Laphroaig.

DIRK. Thank you.

(They clink glasses. They lock eyes, drink.)

(BERT enters, a little stunned.)

Bert!

BERT. Have you seen what's happening to the sky?

DIRK. What's happening to the sky?

BERT. It's turning the strangest color. I've never seen anything
like it. A devastating, confounding color.

(A brief, awkward silence.)

(The doorbell rings.)

DIRK. That must be Celeste and James.

(SANDRA makes a move toward the intercom.)

Let me get it, Sandra.

*(DIRK exits to answer the door. SANDRA and
BERT are alone now.)*

SANDRA. Bertram, what are you trying to do?

BERT. I'm not trying to do anything.

SANDRA. Where did you disappear to?

BERT. I went to the bathroom.

SANDRA. To do what?

BERT. To trim my nose hairs. And then I went to go check on the garden. To make sure the geese...

SANDRA. To make sure the geese what?

BERT. To make sure they weren't...

SANDRA. Weren't what?

> (**BERT** *says nothing. He simply stares at her.*)

Why are you looking at me like that?

BERT. Sandra my love...

SANDRA. What.

BERT. Are we okay?

SANDRA. What a clever thing to ask, Bertram. What a clever, clever thing to ask on a night such as this.

> (**DIRK** *enters with* **CELESTE** *and* **JAMES**. **CELESTE** *is fifty-ish, sweet, wears a light cashmere sweater and pearls. Her beauty is slightly obscured by her shyness.* **JAMES** *is thirty, and despite a clean shave and severely combed hair is a bit forlorn-looking. He rarely makes eye contact with anyone and seems generally haunted. He wears simple pants and a long-sleeved, collared shirt, no tie, soft shoes. He uses a cane and walks with a limp.*)

Celeste!

CELESTE. Hello, Sandra.

SANDRA. You look wonderful!

CELESTE. So do you. Is that Chanel?

SANDRA. It most certainly is.

CELESTE. I love the sparkles.

SANDRA. Your hair.

CELESTE. Do you think it's too much?

SANDRA. Heavens, no. You look divine.

> (*To* **JAMES**.) Hello, James.

JAMES. Hello.

SANDRA. So lovely to see you! Welcome!

> *(They hug stiffly.)*

Bertram, say hello to James.

BERT. Hello, James. So good to see you.

JAMES. You, too, Dr. Cabot.

BERT. You're looking well.

> *(He extends his hand and they shake.)*

Hello, Celeste.

CELESTE. Hi, Bert.

> *(They kiss chastely on the cheek.)*
>
> *(JAMES looks at his hand, a bit abstracted.)*

You okay, honey?

JAMES. Uh-huh.

CELESTE. How's your hip? Did you want some pain stuff? *(To everyone.)* The physical therapy has been helping quite a bit, but he still has some pain.

> *(Awkward pause.)*

BERT. Did anyone see the sky?

DIRK. Bert here was just going on about it.

CELESTE. Wasn't it strange-looking?

BERT. I don't think I've ever seen anything like it.

CELESTE. I kept expecting hail.

JAMES. The cows were huddling.

SANDRA. Cows? What cows?

CELESTE. He's talking about the cows at the Chesterton farm.

DIRK. They huddle when it's about to rain, don't they, son?

JAMES. It's like they're plotting.

SANDRA. Plotting what exactly?

JAMES. Just plots.

> *(Awkward pause.)*

SANDRA. Well, I'm glad everyone made it in one piece. Would anyone care for a drink?

CELESTE. I'll have a glass of red wine, thanks.

SANDRA. Is a Lafite okay?

CELESTE. Ooh, Lafite.

SANDRA. James?

JAMES. Maybe some water.

SANDRA. Sparkling or flat?

CELESTE. Flat is fine, right James? Flat okay?

> (**JAMES** *nods.* **SANDRA** *engages the intercom.*)

SANDRA. *(Into intercom.)* Wilma, could you please come pour Mrs. Von Stofenberg a glass of the Lafite and bring in a carafe of water?
> *(To the room.)* This is going to be a wonderful evening, everyone. I can just feel it.

CELESTE. I love what you've done with the front of the house, by the way.

DIRK. Oh, yeah, the front of the house!

CELESTE. That little garden next to the carport is beautiful. What are those flowers?

SANDRA. Desert roses. Bertram planted them just after the thaw.

CELESTE. I've never heard of desert roses.

BERT. Adenium obesum. They grow all year round.

CELESTE. The colors are exquisite.

> (**WILMA** *enters with a carafe of water, pours a glass from the sideboard, hands it to* **JAMES**.)

JAMES. Thank you.

WILMA. You're welcome.

SANDRA. *(Correcting her.)* De rien.

WILMA. *(To* **JAMES**.*)* De rien.

> (**WILMA** *pours* **CELESTE**'s *glass of wine, hands it to her.*)

CELESTE. *(Out of politeness.)* Merci beaucoup.

WILMA. De rien.

SANDRA. Wilma, this is Celeste Von Stofenberg and her son, James, our Guest of Honor this evening.

WILMA. Nice to meet you.

CELESTE. Nice to meet you, too, Wilma. James?

JAMES. De rien.

SANDRA. Wilma has been with us for a couple of weeks and she's doing excellently, isn't she, Bertram?

BERT. She's doing very well, yes.

SANDRA. *(To* **WILMA.***)* You may start bringing everything out now. Merci beaucoup.

> *(**WILMA** nods, exits.)*
>
> *(**CORA** enters, wearing sandals now. Her hair is up.)*

Glad you could finally join us, Cora. You remember James, right?

CORA. *(To* **JAMES.***)* When the cows huddle they *are* plotting things.

JAMES. What do you think they're plotting?

CORA. How to take down the farmer.

> *(**CORA** and **JAMES** watch each other intensely.)*

SANDRA. Cora, say hello to Mr. and Mrs. Von Stofenberg.

CELESTE. Hi, Cora.

> *(**CORA** "air kisses" **CELESTE** on either cheek, from across the room.)*

DIRK. Hello, Cora. It seems like it's been forever since we've seen you. When was the last time, Christmas?

CORA. Christmas, yes. You left a window open and it snowed in your living room.

DIRK. That's right. It snowed in the living room! Wasn't that something?!

CORA. And then your toilet got backed up because someone tried to flush their tenderloin.

> *(Awkward pause.)*

CELESTE. I just love your hair like that, Cora.

CORA. I was going to cut it all off but I was afraid James wouldn't recognize me.

DIRK. You recognize Cora, right James?

(**JAMES** *nods.*)

BERT. Would you like a glass of wine, honey?

CORA. Yes, please.

(**BERT** *pours her a glass, hands it to her.*)

BERT. I'd like to propose a toast.

(*Lifting his glass.*) To James. Welcome home.

DIRK. Hear, hear. Welcome home, Son.

CELESTE. And to new beginnings.

DIRK. Hear, hear!

CORA. (*Looking at* **JAMES**.) And to the huddling cows.

DIRK. To the huddling cows. Hear, hear!

(*They all clink glasses.*)

SANDRA. Shall we sit?

CELESTE. That would be great. Where would you like us?

SANDRA. I'll sit at the end by the window. Bertram will sit next to me. Opposite him will be Dirk and Celeste. Cora, darling, you can sit here.

BERT. And tonight, our Guest of Honor, James, sits at the head of the table.

DIRK. Let's get to it!

(*They all take their seats.*)

(**CORA** *starts to hum a tone with her mouth closed, barely audible. Everyone looks about, confused, including* **CORA**.)

SANDRA. Who's doing that?

(*It continues.*)

DIRK. Is that coming from the kitchen?

*(It goes on for another moment. **SANDRA** rises and is about to press a button on the intercom when **CORA** starts laughing, exposing herself as the culprit.)*

CELESTE. Cora, that was you?

DIRK. I honestly thought it was coming from the kitchen.

CORA. Or the basement.

SANDRA. *(To **CORA**.)* Mischievous little raccoon.

*(**SANDRA** returns to the table, sits.)*

CELESTE. Sandra, this tableware is stunning. What is it?

SANDRA. It's English Onslow by Wallace.

CELESTE. I just love it.

SANDRA. We've been quite pleased with it. Do be careful with the knife. It's much sharper than it looks. The spoon, too.

CORA. The first utensils were made of bone. You kept them on your person everywhere you went.

DIRK. That's fascinating, Cora.

CORA. In addition to eating, they were also used to core out the eyes of sleeping enemies.

BERT. Cora, honey.

*(**WILMA** enters with a large dish, sets it on the table.)*

Wow. Would you look at that!

CELESTE. It looks wonderful! What is it?

SANDRA. Wild goose.

CELESTE. Wild goose! How exciting! How is it prepared?

SANDRA. It's slow cooked in its own juices.

CELESTE. I didn't see any wild geese at the market.

SANDRA. This wild goose isn't from the market.

CELESTE. Oh. Did you go to Litchfield for it?

SANDRA. It's special ordered actually.

(Awkward pause.)

DIRK. Here's to the goose!

CELESTE. To the goose!

SANDRA. Here's to James!

DIRK. To James!

CELESTE. Cheers everyone!

> *(Everyone says "Cheers!" and clinks glasses.* **WILMA** *returns with a large plate of scalloped potatoes prepared in truffle oil and a plate of asparagus. People start serving themselves.* **WILMA** *exits again and returns with a large serving bowl of salad. She sets it down, exits.)*

SANDRA. Cora, are your hands washed?

> *(***CORA*** *doesn't answer.)*

BERT. Cora?

> *(***CORA*** *holds her hands up for everyone to see, then lowers them.)*

SANDRA. So, Celeste, how have things been with you? Are you still volunteering at the foundling hospital?

CELESTE. I'm afraid not.

DIRK. The drive to Norwich was getting so tedious.

CELESTE. Oh, I didn't mind the drive at all. I could handle the drive just fine.

CORA. They lost their funding.

SANDRA. What a shame.

CORA. They had all their money invested with what's his face.

BERT. Well, that's tragic.

SANDRA. So what happens to all those children?

CELESTE. Well, they found other centers for most of them. Wherever there was room.

SANDRA. But what about the others?

CELESTE. No one knows.

JAMES. They got lost again.

CORA. The unlucky ones.

DIRK. Maybe they're huddling with the cows...

> *(This falls flat.)*

Bad joke. Sorry.

CELESTE. I certainly miss them. All those sweet little faces.

BERT. I can't imagine it, Celeste.

CELESTE. I mean, who in their right mind would abandon their own infant child?

SANDRA. We live in a brutal world of often marginal consequences.

> *(Awkward pause.)*

DIRK. Honey, tell them about your story.

CELESTE. Oh, I wouldn't want to bore them.

BERT. Bore us? That's nonsense, Celeste.

SANDRA. What's this story?

DIRK. She's been working on a children's book.

BERT. How wonderful!

CELESTE. It's nothing, really.

DIRK. At least tell them what it's called, honey.

CELESTE. It's called *Ainsley Asbury Learns to Fly.*

BERT. It sounds fascinating. What's it about?

CELESTE. You really want to know?

SANDRA. Celeste, if you don't tell us about it I'm going to have to banish you to the basement.

CELESTE. Well, in that case... It's about a little boy named Ainsley Asbury whose parents abandon him in the bottom of a dead, uncharted volcano while on vacation in Hawaii. He's befriended by a baby pterodactyl named Clyde who is lost in the wrong century and searching for a time machine. Clyde and Ainsley survive together. Clyde forages outside of the volcano for food and feeds Ainsley with his beak. And because the volcano is on the Island of Maui, which is such a thriving, tropical part of Hawaii, Clyde is able to bring back the finest fruits and vegetables.

Eventually, Clyde teaches Ainsley how to fly. But because Ainsley is so well provided for he starts putting on too much weight and flying higher becomes harder and harder.

SANDRA. So Ainsley grows up to be a tub of lard. And then what?

JAMES. He has to sacrifice part of himself.

BERT. In what way?

CELESTE. Oh, this is so embarrassing.

JAMES. He has to cut off part of his body.

SANDRA. How perfectly grisly! What part?!

CELESTE. Well, I was thinking his –

JAMES. Feet.

CELESTE. ...Feet...because they're so large, but I can't get past the fact that he would have no real way of getting around outside of the volcano.

SANDRA. But wouldn't that be part of the sacrifice? Self-inflicted injury? How wonderfully Greek!

DIRK. He'd probably bleed to death.

JAMES. Not if Clyde cauterized the wounds.

SANDRA. Cauterized them how, James?

JAMES. With fire and stones. Or molten lava.

CELESTE. I suppose there could still be a bit of active lava somewhere.

(*Beat.*)

SANDRA. What do you suppose they'd use to cut off young Ainsley's feet?

CELESTE. You know, whenever I get to that part I get so sleepy and I just can't seem to finish it.

DIRK. Well, you will, honey. You really will. We all have faith in you.

BERT. *Ainsley Asbury Learns to Fly.* It's a wonderful title, Celeste. I can't wait to read it.

SANDRA. Is Ainsley a boy's name? A trifling detail, I realize.

CELESTE. Oh my god, is Ainsley strictly a girl's name?

SANDRA. You might want to double-check. It could be confusing.

(*Awkward pause.*)

JAMES. There was this guy at Stockbridge named Cheryl.

SANDRA. (*Mostly to herself.*) Well, that's disgusting.

JAMES. He told everyone he was Mexican.

DIRK. Was he?

JAMES. No, he was rich and white. Like us. And he had herpes on his arms.

CORA. Maybe he was Mexican on the inside.

(*Awkward pause.*)

BERT. Your story really does sound fascinating, Celeste.

CELESTE. Well, tonight the real story is that James is home.

DIRK. Hear, hear!

BERT. Hear, hear!

(*They clink glasses and drink. They eat in silence.*)

DIRK. Sandra, I must say that this wild goose is just delicious.

SANDRA. Why thank you, Dirk!

CELESTE. And the potatoes! How are they prepared?

SANDRA. DaRosario white truffle oil.

CELESTE. White truffle oil. How yummy!

SANDRA. Wait till you see dessert.

DIRK. What is it?

SANDRA. It's a surprise. I practically had to go to the ends of the earth to find the main ingredient.

CELESTE. Ooh, mystery dessert, how exciting! I can't wait!

DIRK. A toast to the chef!

(*They all say "Cheers!" and clink glasses again.*)

CELESTE. Cora, what about you? Do you have any big plans for the summer?

(**CORA** *simply stares at* **CELESTE**. *Not threatening. Just a stare.*)

BERT. Cora's been working on a project.

CELESTE. Like an art project?

CORA. It's more metaphysical in nature.

CELESTE. What are your materials?

CORA. Human arm hair and construction paper. Plus whatever viscous adhesive that makes itself readily available.

CELESTE. It sounds so mysterious.

CORA. Every hair makes a difference.

SANDRA. Does it now, Cora?

CORA. No hair shall be left behind.

(*Awkward pause.*)

BERT. What about you, James, what are your immediate plans?

JAMES. I don't really have any.

CELESTE. Well, you just got that job at the high school.

SANDRA. At Choate?

CELESTE. At the public school.

SANDRA. Oh. How nice. Doing what, exactly?

DIRK. Polishing the gymnasium floor, right, Son?

CELESTE. They're re-doing the floor in the fieldhouse and they needed someone to operate one of those oscillating machines.

DIRK. Which James learned how to use at Stockbridge.

SANDRA. When do you start?

JAMES. In a few weeks. But I was maybe thinking about traveling.

SANDRA. Traveling where?

JAMES. I'd like to go to Iraq.

SANDRA. Iraq.

CELESTE. While he was at Stockbridge, James started a correspondence with a young Iraqi boy. What was his name?

JAMES. Malik.

CELESTE. Malik, right.

DIRK. You met online, right Son?

CELESTE. Stockbridge has a wonderful new media center.

SANDRA. How old is Malik?

JAMES. Fourteen.

SANDRA. Is he in school?

JAMES. No.

SANDRA. Well, then how does he correspond with you?

JAMES. He has a computer.

SANDRA. I was under the impression that most Iraqi children were destitute.

JAMES. His Movement gave him the computer.

SANDRA. His *Movement*?

DIRK. It's a Freedom Movement, Sandra.

 (*To* **JAMES.**) It's a Freedom Movement, right, Son?

JAMES. You could call it that.

SANDRA. What does Rahim do for this Movement?

JAMES. Malik. He mostly makes stuff.

BERT. What kind of stuff?

JAMES. Blankets. Water filters. Makeshift explosives. I try and help out any way I can.

BERT. In what way?

JAMES. I provide information.

SANDRA. And how does one provide this kind of information?

JAMES. Oh, there's all kinds of stuff on the Internet. And you can learn a lot from manuals.

SANDRA. Can't Hakeem go on the Internet?

JAMES. Malik. Sure, but our government regulates their servers. In order to get anything done I have to write emails in code.

SANDRA. You're writing to a terrorist *in code*?

CELESTE. He's not a terrorist, Sandra, he's just a boy. A regular Iraqi boy who happens to have a computer, right James?

DIRK. Sandra, there's really no reason to be alarmed.

JAMES. I have a picture of him if you guys want to see it. It's drawn with keyboard characters but it looks like a fourteen-year-old Iraqi insurgent to me. You should see his `imama.

SANDRA. What's an `imama?

JAMES. His turban. It's really beautiful.

CELESTE. But it's a *Freedom* Movement, right Jamie?

JAMES. Freedom, sure.

> *(Awkward pause.)*

BERT. Anyone care for more wine?

CELESTE. I'd love some, Bert, thanks.

> **(BERT** *starts for the intercom.* **SANDRA** *beats him to it.)*

SANDRA. *(Into intercom.)* Wilma, be a dear and bring out another bottle of the Lafite please.
> *(To* **CORA.***)* Cora, stop staring at James, it's not polite.

> **(WILMA** *enters with another decanted bottle of the Lafite, sets it on the table.)*

Merci, Wilma.

WILMA. De rien, Madame.

> **(WILMA** *exits.)*

> **(BERT** *pours* **CELESTE** *a glass of wine. They share a look.)*

> **(SANDRA** *crosses to the window.)*

SANDRA. Bertram it looks as if your purported sickly sky has moved into our backyard. My *god*, is that beige?

> *(All move to the window and peer out, except for* **CORA** *and* **JAMES.***)*

BERT. Do you see those streaks?

CELESTE. Is that aurora borealis?

DIRK. Do we even get that in America?

CELESTE. James, honey, come look at the sky.

> **(JAMES** *doesn't move.)*

SANDRA. Cora...

CORA. (*Staring at* **JAMES**.) I can see it from here.

CELESTE. What's going on out there?

DIRK. Huh...

>(**SANDRA** *draws the curtains closed.*)

SANDRA. Let's sit, shall we?

>(*They all make their way back to the table.*)

Has everyone had enough to eat? There's plenty more.

DIRK. I'm stuffed.

CELESTE. I'd like to save some room for the mystery dessert.

SANDRA. James?

JAMES. No thanks.

SANDRA. So we're all stuffed to the gills. Excellent.

>(*She crosses to the intercom, presses a button.*)

(*Into intercom.*) Wilma, will you begin clearing the table, please?

CELESTE. The food was just so good, Sandra.

SANDRA. (*Sitting.*) Oh, Celeste, you're too kind.

>(**JAMES** *stands suddenly, jarring the table. The plates, silverware, etc. jump. All freeze.*)

JAMES. May I use your bathroom?

SANDRA. Of course. It's through those doors, down the hall and on your right.

>(**JAMES** *exits.*)

BERT. He seems like he's doing very well.

CELESTE. It hasn't been easy, but he's showing signs.

DIRK. He's been spending a lot of time in the woods behind the house.

SANDRA. What's he doing?

DIRK. Just taking long walks.

CELESTE. Dr. Gentry thinks nature's a good thing.

BERT. How could it not be?

> (**WILMA** *enters, grabs a few plates, exits. Returns immediately, takes another two plates, starts to exit.*)

SANDRA. Wilma?

WILMA. Oui, Madame.

SANDRA. Un sonnet, s'il vous plaît? You can set those dishes on the sideboard.

WILMA. Oui, Madame.

> (*She sets the dishes on the sideboard, takes a position where everyone can see her, stands very straight, recites the following sonnet with a perfect, mid-Atlantic accent:*)

In the old age black was not counted fair,
Or if it were, it bore not beauty's name;
But now is black beauty's successive heir,
And beauty slandered with a bastard shame:
For since each hand hath put on Nature's power,
Fairing the foul with Art's false borrowed face,
Sweet beauty hath no name, no holy bower,
But is profaned, if not lives in disgrace.
Therefore my mistress' eyes are raven black,
Her eyes so suited, and they mourners seem
At such who, not born fair, no beauty lack,
Sland'ring creation with a false esteem:
Yet so they mourn becoming of their woe,
That every tongue says beauty should look *so*.

SANDRA. Bravo, Wilma! Magnifique!

> (**SANDRA** *leads applause.*)

WILMA. Merci. Merci beaucoup.

DIRK. That was wonderful! Encore!

WILMA. Merci.

DIRK. Was that Shakespeare?

WILMA. Oui, Monsieur.

BERT. He would be proud.

SANDRA. Perhaps she'll grace us with another one during dessert.

DIRK. I would just *love* that!

CELESTE. Do you know any about flying?

CORA. No, but she knows a few about falling, right Wilma?

WILMA. Oui, Madame.

DIRK. What do you mean by falling?

CORA. Falling in love, Dirk.

SANDRA. That's Mr. Von Stofenberg to you, Cora.

DIRK. She can call me Dirk, Sandra, I don't mind.

CORA. I've always liked the name Dirk. It sounds like a plate breaking.

> *(She holds up a plate and lets it fall to the floor. After it breaks:)*

See? Dirk.

> *(**JAMES** enters.)*

JAMES. You have really nice soap.

SANDRA. I'm glad you like it, James.

JAMES. Soap's important.

BERT. It certainly is.

> *(**JAMES** sits.)*

SANDRA. You may continue clearing, Wilma.

WILMA. Oui, Madame.

> *(**WILMA** gathers the pieces of the broken plate. **BERT** helps her.)*

SANDRA. Would anyone care to see the basement?

CELESTE. I'd love to see it. The other day Dirk was just telling me how you've recently renovated.

SANDRA. We're quite proud of what's happening down there, aren't we Bertram?

BERT. *(Somewhere else.)* Huh?

SANDRA. I'm talking about the basement and how pleased we are with the renovations. I was going to show our guests.

BERT. Oh, the basement, yes. We're pleased...

> *(To* **CORA***.)* Cora, honey, what does my name sound like? Bert.

CORA. Like the noise the farmer makes when the cows take him down at the slaughterhouse. Bert. Bolt to the brain. Kerplunk.

> *(***BERT** *almost falls.* **JAMES** *catches him, helps him steady himself.)*

DIRK. Whoa there. Easy now, Bert.

> *(They all stand back.* **BERT** *regains his composure.* **WILMA** *takes the remaining piece of broken plate from him, exits.)*

You okay, buddy?

BERT. Thank you, James... I love you, Cora.

CORA. I love you too, Daddy.

CELESTE. Would you like a glass of water, Bert?

BERT. I'm fine, Celeste.

SANDRA. Shall we?

> *(She leads them off to the basement.* **CELESTE** *and* **BERT** *exit.* **WILMA** *enters, clears more dishes from the table.)*

Wilma, you may begin preparing the after-dinner digestif.

WILMA. Oui, Madame.

SANDRA. Cora? James?

CORA. I already know what's down there.

JAMES. The stairs aren't so good for my hip.

SANDRA. Well, if you need anything, just use the intercom and let Wilma know.

> *(***SANDRA** *and* **DIRK** *exit.* **WILMA** *continues to clear dishes. A long silence between* **CORA** *and* **JAMES.** **WILMA** *exits. Then:)*

CORA. Are you glad to be home?

JAMES. I guess.

CORA. I was in Cambridge when my dad called to tell me you'd jumped. I was impressed. That takes courage.

> *(Awkward pause.)*

You can look at me.

> *(**JAMES** continues looking down.)*

Am I that ugly?

JAMES. No.

CORA. James, look at me.

> *(**JAMES** finally looks.)*

Hi.

JAMES. Hi.

CORA. I thought you'd come back with gray hair... You still have such a nice face. I've always thought that. Even when your arms were really skinny and you had impetigo.

JAMES. I'm sure I'll get gray hair soon enough.

> *(He stands to clear his plate, as does **CORA**. **WILMA** enters, takes their dishes.)*

CORA. What have you been doing in the woods behind your house?

JAMES. What?

CORA. Your dad just told us you'd been spending a lot of time there.

JAMES. I just like the trees and stuff. There's a stream. Sometimes you see animals.

CORA. What kind of animals?

JAMES. Deer mostly. Deer and birds. And there's this fox... I touched one the other day.

CORA. A fox?

JAMES. A deer. Walked right up to it and touched its face. It felt like velvet. Its eyes were so brown.

CORA. Do you still hear voices?

JAMES. Sometimes.

CORA. Didn't Stockbridge help?

JAMES. Yeah, but I stopped taking my meds.

CORA. Why?

JAMES. I don't like how they make me feel.

CORA. What were you on?

JAMES. Thorazine and Lithium. Haldol before that.

CORA. What's Haldol like?

JAMES. Like being half-asleep in a snowdrift.

CORA. Does anyone know you stopped taking them?

JAMES. Malik knows.

CORA. You two are pretty close, huh?

JAMES. He's my best friend.

CORA. Are you really going to Iraq?

JAMES. I'm gonna try.

> *(Beat.)*

CORA. I wish I heard voices.

> *(**JAMES** reaches into his pocket, hands her a small soap sculpture of a goose.)*

Where'd you get this?

JAMES. From the bathroom. It's a goose. At first I thought it might be a swan but it's clearly a goose. You can tell by the neck. You can keep it.

CORA. Thanks, James, that's really sweet.

> *(She opens her pouch, places the soap in it.)*

Is it true what your manager at Walmart said in the paper? That you'd been stealing stuffed animals and hiding them in a supply closet.

JAMES. They're the ones who told me I could fly. Butterscotch Pony and Barbie Island Princess Monkey Plush were the ringleaders.

CORA. What exactly did they say to you?

JAMES. That I didn't need a car anymore because I had the gift of flight.

CORA. So Butterscotch Pony and Barbie Island Princess Monkey Plush lied to you.

JAMES. Yeah, if I've learned anything it's that it's pretty important not to trust stuffed animals. Especially those two.

> *(Pause.)*

CORA. I rarely leave the house. I mostly stay in my room... "What's your room like?" he asks, trying not to look at her from across the table. "Lots of books stacked everywhere," she replies. "Four-poster bed. Orange peels here and there. Big plastic bag of pennies." "What's your favorite book?" he then queries, self-consciously playing with his silverware. "*Where The Wild Things Are*," she answers, relieved that the conversation is finally gaining momentum.

JAMES. That's about that kid in the wolf costume. The jungle grows in his room.

CORA. And then the monsters come.

> *(**JAMES** nods.)*

I think it's one of the most important pieces of literature ever written. The author originally envisioned horses instead of monsters but he couldn't draw them well enough. What's your favorite book?

JAMES. *Old Yeller.*

CORA. That's about the dog, right? They shoot him because he gets sick.

JAMES. He actually gets bitten by a rabid wolf when he's defending his adoptive family. And they have to put him down.

CORA. Because he turns into a monster.

JAMES. Yeah, I like that book a lot.

> *(Beat.)*

CORA. So did you really think you could fly or were you just that unhappy?

(**JAMES** *reaches into his pocket, gives her another soap miniature.*)

JAMES. Another goose.

(**CORA** *accepts it, places it in her pouch.*)

CORA. James, can I have some of your arm hair for my art project? You can say no, I won't be offended.

JAMES. Why do you need people's arm hair?

CORA. Because I'm making a magic beard. That you can wear. To disappear.

JAMES. How does that work?

CORA. You put it on and literally disappear.

JAMES. Where do you go?

CORA. You appear in the dreams of all the people who gave you their arm hair.

JAMES. You like haunt them?

CORA. Haunt. Visit. Torture... Flirt.

JAMES. So if my arm hair was part of the beard and you wore it I would dream about you?

(**CORA** *nods.*)

Would you be actually wearing the arm hair beard in my dream?

CORA. Very likely, yes.

JAMES. That would be weird.

CORA. Maybe. But it could be fun.

JAMES. What would we do?

CORA. I don't know. I imagine whatever we'd care to.

(**JAMES** *is embarrassed.*)

Every arm hair counts and I have a ways to go, James Emory Von Stofenberg, so can I have some?

JAMES. What's your middle name?

CORA. Fawn.

JAMES. Like the deer.

CORA. That's me: the family deer.

> (**JAMES** *moves to her, touches her face.*)

May I?

> (**JAMES** *nods.* **CORA** *unbuttons his sleeve, bares his forearm. She then removes the small, velvet sack that is tied around her waist, undoes it, regards* **JAMES'** *arm for a moment, then very quickly pulls out some hair.* **JAMES** *winces, but just barely.* **CORA** *places the bit of arm hair in her bag, closes it, re-wraps it around her waist. This action has somehow unlocked* **CORA.** *She takes* **JAMES** *by the shoulder, squares his body to hers. She looks at him intensely, then kisses him. It triples in intensity. She jumps on him and they start lurching around the room, ravishing each other, quickly, with animal intensity. They wind up on the dining room table,* **CORA** *shedding her underwear,* **JAMES** *somehow getting his pants down.* **CORA** *mounts* **JAMES** *on the table.* **WILMA** *enters.*)

WILMA. Oh, hell no, Cora!

> (**CORA** *guides* **JAMES'** *penis into her. Astonishing pleasure. They start making love, creating quite a mess.* **WILMA** *has to do everything she can to clean up after them. Place settings fly. Wine bottles topple.* **WILMA** *expertly polices most of these small potential disasters. During* **WILMA'S** *policing,* **JAMES** *accidentally grabs her, pulls her into the fray.* **WILMA** *wrests herself away.* **CORA** *and* **JAMES** *are nearing climax now. Perhaps three titanic bursts. They both orgasm and* **CORA** *collapses on top of* **JAMES.** **WILMA** *gives them a moment and then gently hurries them off the table and fixes things just as they were.*)

> (*Voices can be heard coming from the basement.* **CORA** *finds her underwear, rushes into them,*

fixes her hair. **JAMES** *fixes his pants. They take their original seats at the table, a bit out of breath, exhilarated.)*

(Moments later, the rest of the party enters. **CORA** *and* **JAMES** *stand, breathing heavily, trying to hide it.)*

DIRK. *(Offstage.)* It doesn't smell like a basement at all down there.

CELESTE. *(Offstage.)* It smells like freshly fallen snow.

(The four adults enter.)

DIRK. Sandra and Bert, I'm so impressed. I had no idea it was so elaborate down there.

CELESTE. That must have taken months.

SANDRA. We hired the best contractors money could buy.

DIRK. The team from Kent or Greenwich?

SANDRA. Milford, actually.

CELESTE. Milford! Who would've thought?

DIRK. The meditation room!

CELESTE. And the gymnasium.

DIRK. That parquet floor is just beautiful.

CELESTE. And the billiards annex.

DIRK. The sauna!

CELESTE. And that aquarium!

DIRK. That's a real barracuda?

SANDRA. All forty-seven inches of him.

DIRK. Forty-seven inches! Son of a gun!

SANDRA. He was caught in the Paradise Reef in Cozumel, Mexico.

CELESTE. How did you find it, if you don't mind me asking?

SANDRA. We know a dealer.

BERT. Man from Cornwall. Odd, odd man.

SANDRA. But he certainly knows how to find you a fish.

DIRK. What do you feed it?

SANDRA. Other fish.

BERT. We have an arrangement with a fisherman from Norwalk. Comes by every few weeks.

SANDRA. He brings us perch, croppy, small-mouthed bass. In exchange we pay him a little money, invite him in for a drink –

CORA. And let him do bong hits in the gazebo.

SANDRA. We do nothing of the sort!

BERT. He does like the gazebo. But I think those are clove cigarettes you're smelling, Cora.

CORA. I caught him whacking off the other day.

BERT. Cora –

CORA. There are cum stains all over the gazebo, go see for yourself. He was whacking off and doing bong hits.

DIRK. *(A joke.)* As long as he keeps feeding that big fish!

(Laughter all around.)

CELESTE. And how about the screening room? *We* should do that, Dirk.

SANDRA. The sound system is state of the art. I say why even *go* to the movies when you can achieve a better experience in the comfort of your own home?

DIRK. It certainly makes sense.

CORA. *(To* **DIRK.***)* So did you see it?

SANDRA. See what, Cora?

CORA. What else is in the basement.

SANDRA. He saw everything in the basement, we just *returned* from there.

CORA. *(To* **DIRK.***)* You didn't see what was behind the little door in the far wall?

SANDRA. What little door? There's no little door.

CORA. It's the same color as the wall. Because it's not meant to be seen.
(To **DIRK.***)* If you crouch low enough you can hear it preening its paws.

SANDRA. You're being ridiculous, Cora. Stop playing games and sit down.

(CORA remains standing for a moment, challenging her mother a bit, then slowly sits.)

Would anyone care for a Pink Squirrel or a Tequila Sunrise? Bertram and I just procured a bottle of the finest grenadine on the market. I could make a Roy Rogers or a Shirley Temple, if you'd prefer something softer.

(Looking at DIRK.*)* This particular bottle of grenadine came from the finest Himalayan pomegranates. Celeste?

CELESTE. Oh, I've always wanted to try a pink squirrel.

SANDRA. Coming right up. James?

JAMES. No thanks.

SANDRA. Bertram?

BERT. I'll try a Roy Rogers. Just to taste the stuff.

SANDRA. Dirk? As I said, this grenadine happens to come from the finest Himalayan pomegranates.

DIRK. Oh! Of course! I mean sure, I'll try a splash of it!

SANDRA. Hard or soft?

DIRK. Hard. I mean soft! I mean hard! I mean soft!

SANDRA. Roy Rogers?

DIRK. Yes, a Roy Rogers! Perfect!

(SANDRA engages the intercom.)

SANDRA. *(Into intercom.)* Wilma, could you please bring in that tray of drinks?

(WILMA enters with a tray of glasses containing ginger ale, Coca-Cola, and a cocktail shaker containing crème de noyaux, white crème de cacao, and heavy cream. She sets it on the sideboard.)

CORA. *(To* DIRK.*)* It really is down there.

SANDRA. Cora Michaela Cabot that's enough!

CORA. My middle name's not Michaela, it's Fawn.

SANDRA. Bertram, will you please talk some sense into your daughter?

BERT. Cora, honey, come on now.

*(**SANDRA** successfully makes **BERT**'s Roy Rogers, hands it to him. She then makes one for **DIRK**, hands it to him – the identical drink. She starts to add grenadine to the cocktail mixer to make **CELESTE** her pink squirrel when she knocks over the ice cube container, making a big scene.)*

SANDRA. Oh, dear, what a mess I've made! My Chanel!

*(There is much hustling to help her. **BERT** sets his Roy Rogers on the table quickly, moves to help her, as does **CELESTE**, as does **JAMES**, who nearly falls. **CORA** stops his fall.)*

*(**DIRK** sets his Roy Rogers down, removes the vial from his pocket, and empties it into Bert's Roy Rogers. **SANDRA** and **DIRK** make eye contact. And then **DIRK** joins the others, attempting to help **SANDRA** with her mess.)*

(To all.) Oh, I'm such a klutz. I'm so sorry, everyone.

*(**WILMA** exits to the kitchen, then re-enters, takes over the cleaning duties.)*

Thank you, Wilma.

(Everyone returns to their places at the table.)

Shall we have the salad?

*(**SANDRA** crosses to **JAMES** with the salad bowl. **JAMES** takes the salad bowl, serves himself, passes it to **CELESTE**, who does the same. **DIRK** is suddenly confused about what Roy Rogers he has poured the liquid into. He switches his and Bert's glasses, then switches them back, then switches them again. **SANDRA** then switches them yet a final time.)*

DIRK. Germs... I've been fighting something off all night.

(Forces a cough.)

Sorry, Bert.

SANDRA. This is the one you drank from, Dirk.

CELESTE. Honey, I brought the Esberitox. Would you like some?

DIRK. Later maybe. When we get home.

> *(He fakes another cough, swallows, drinks from his Roy Rogers.)*

There, that's better. Wow, that's good! Yum!

> *(Beat.* **BERT** *is about to drink from his Roy Rogers.)*

CELESTE. Bert, the other day, Dirk was telling me that you recently received a special honor.

BERT. *(Setting his glass down.)* Yeah, a couple of people thought my work as an osteopath was something to make a little fuss about.

CELESTE. That's wonderful.

BERT. It was really no big deal. There was a banquet in New York and they gave me a hunk of Lucite and a pat on the back. It's all a bit sentimental, really.

CELESTE. Well, congratulations. I'm sure it's well deserved.

BERT. Thank you, Celeste.

SANDRA. *(Raising her wine glass.)* To a long and fruitful career.

CELESTE. To Bert.

DIRK. To Bert! Cheers!

> *(They all raise their glasses to toast. Just as* **BERT** *is about to drink, the sudden loud sound of the house being attacked. Several thuds detonate against the house. Again,* **BERT** *sets his glass down. Everyone stands.)*

CELESTE. Was that hail?

SANDRA. Wilma, dear, will you go see what that was?

WILMA. *(Still cleaning.)* Oui, Madame.

> *(***SANDRA*** *stands, turns, and peers out the window.* **DIRK** *is transfixed by Bert's glass, suddenly somewhere else, abstracted.)*

SANDRA. It's too dark to make anything out.

(*Looking at her Rolex.*) The yard lamps don't turn on for another few minutes.

JAMES. Dad...

(**DIRK** *doesn't answer.*)

Dad...

CELESTE. Dirk?

DIRK. Huh.

CELESTE. Are you okay?

DIRK. I was just thinking...

CELESTE. About what, honey?

DIRK. About how we suddenly...*arrive* places. How so often we can be nowhere and then just suddenly *arrive*... like...like we're traveling but asleep...like in the back of a car when you're a child...lying in the way back on an old wool blanket...the sound of voices in the front seat. Or the radio...Kenny Delmar on the radio.

Look at us. We're all here, gathered around this table, and anything could happen...like that thing going on in the sky, and whatever it was that just hit the side of the house...or what if the barracuda grew legs and walked up here from the basement and started demanding things...and we all got stuck...like our legs and our hands and our faces...the barracuda could walk right up to the table here and start demanding things but we wouldn't be able to move.

(**WILMA** *returns, holding a dead Canadian goose, the neck broken.*)

CELESTE. Oh my god.

SANDRA. How many are there, Wilma?

WILMA. Twenty, maybe thirty. Shall I take it to the basement?

SANDRA. Yes, get rid of all of them, please.

WILMA. Oui, Madame.

(*She exits with the dead goose.*)

SANDRA. *(To everyone.)* We've recently acquired a sort of all-purpose garbage disposal. I didn't show it on the tour because it's rather boring-looking.

CELESTE. Is it an incinerator?

SANDRA. It's a garbage disposal. State of the art. The finest one available on the market. It cost us thousands.

> *(**BERT** rises.)*

Where are you going?

BERT. To the garden.

SANDRA. Why?

BERT. Because I want to make sure there aren't any of those geese eating our flowers.

SANDRA. Sit down please.

BERT. No.

SANDRA. Bertram, we have guests –

> *(**BERT** exits.)*
>
> *(**WILMA** enters, holding two more geese. One is alive.)*

WILMA. Some of them are still alive, Madame.

SANDRA. Well then the sooner we put them out of their misery the better.

WILMA. Oui, Madame.

CELESTE. Those poor geese. What do you even say when something like that happens?

SANDRA. You say nothing, Celeste. You simply sit and say nothing.

> *(They all sit in silence. Perhaps for an uncomfortably long time.)*
>
> *(**BERT** re-enters with a bouquet of cherry and white desert roses that he picked from the garden, hands the bouquet to **CELESTE**.)*

BERT. *(To **CELESTE**.)* Tired with all these, for restful death I cry,
As, to behold desert a beggar born,

And needy nothing trimm'd in jollity,
And purest faith unhappily forsworn,
And guilded honour shamefully misplaced,
And maiden virtue rudely strumpeted,
And right perfection wrongfully disgraced,
And strength by limping sway disabled,
And art made tongue-tied by authority,
And folly doctor-like controlling skill,
And simple truth miscall'd simplicity,
And captive good attending captain ill:
Tired with all these, from these would I be gone,
Save that, to die, I leave my love alone.

CELESTE. Is that Shakespeare, too?

BERT. Sonnet Sixty-six.

CELESTE. It's lovely.

BERT. *(To* **SANDRA**.*)* It's lovely because it's about love.
(To **CELESTE**.*)* And I offer it to you, Celeste, because you're a lovely woman.

CELESTE. I'm touched, Bert.

BERT. Dirk, you're a lucky man.

SANDRA. Please sit down and finish your cocktail, Bertram.

(**BERT** *sits, starts to reach for his Roy Rogers.)*

DIRK. Bert, do you remember the fight song?

BERT. *(Stops reaching for his cocktail glass.)* The fight song?

DIRK. From Yale.

BERT. Of course.

DIRK. Would you mind singing it for me?

BERT. Um, sure. Why?

DIRK. Just sing it for me. I think it would do me a world of good.

BERT. Okay.

(**BERT** *clears his throat. Then, singing simply:)*

BULLDOG BULLDOG

BOW, WOW, WOW
ELI YALE
BULLDOG BULLDOG
BOW, WOW, WOW
OUR TEAM CAN NEVER FAIL

(**JAMES** *suddenly joins in.*)

JAMES. *(Singing simply.)*
WHEN THE SONS OF ELI
BREAK THROUGH THE LINE
THIS IS THE SIGN WE HAIL

JAMES & BERT. *(Singing simply.)*
BULLDOG BULLDOG
BOW, WOW, WOW
ELI YALE

(**DIRK** *suddenly seizes* **BERT**'s *Roy Rogers, gulps it down.*)

DIRK. You were a great coxswain, Bert.

BERT. Thanks, buddy.

DIRK. The absolute best.

(**SANDRA** *stands abruptly.*)

CELESTE. Sandra, what's wrong?

(**SANDRA** *is frozen.*)

Dirk, are you okay?

DIRK. *(To* **SANDRA**.*)* In the dream, while I'm sinking into the lava, another version of me appears, naked, ten-feet tall, walking on the molten rock. He has wings. Enormous, beautiful butterfly wings. And as I can feel my body burning he reaches out to me. He says, "Go on, take my hand, Dirk. Take it." His voice is perfect and soothing. I know he can save me but I'm too afraid...to take his hand... I'm too afraid.

(He rises from the table, a bit disoriented.)

CELESTE. Dirk, honey...

DIRK. I'm fine, sweetheart. Just fine. I'm afraid I'm feeling a bit sleepy. A nap will do me good.

*(He kisses **CELESTE**'s forehead, then her lips. He then moves to **JAMES**, hugs him from behind, buries his head in his shoulder, weeps. After a moment, he stands, regains his composure, exits. The sound of the front door closing.)*

CELESTE. He's been under such a strain lately... All the innuendo... All the funny looks... We don't even feel welcome at the club anymore.

BERT. You're wonderful to stand by him the way you do, Celeste.

CELESTE. It amazes me how people can just turn on you. It really is amazing.

> *(**SANDRA** is turned toward the bay window now.)*

SANDRA. The yard lamps have come on... Dirk's out there.

JAMES. What's he doing?

SANDRA. He's walking toward the weeping willow... He's gazing up at it as if it's the most beautiful thing he's ever seen... And now he's lying down... He's taken his shoes off and he's simply lying underneath the weeping willow.

CELESTE. Should we maybe get him a pillow?

> *(**SANDRA** says nothing, her hand gently touching the window.)*

Sandra?

SANDRA. No. No pillow, Celeste.

> *(**WILMA** enters, holding two more dead geese.)*

WILMA. Madame, the dessert is almost ready.

CORA. Tell them what it is, Sandra.

SANDRA. *(To **CORA**.)* What did you say to me?

CORA. I said tell them what the dessert is.

SANDRA. It's crème brûlée. Made with lion's milk.

WILMA. *(To **SANDRA**.)* Shall I bring it out, Madame?

SANDRA. No. No, thank you, Wilma. I think we've all had enough tonight.

(**WILMA** *exits.*)

(**CORA** *rises and crosses to* **JAMES**, *whispers something in his ear. He rises, exits.*)

(*Silence.*)

(**JAMES** *enters, carrying a dead she-lion, wrapped in a blanket. It is grotesquely arranged, with chains hanging from its limbs. It takes him a great effort, but he carries it to the end of the table, lays it down, in front of Sandra's chair. He crosses to* **SANDRA**, *who is still at the window, takes her hand, leads her to the she-lion, places both of her hands on its body, returns to his chair at the head of the table, sits.* **SANDRA** *starts to feel the body of the lion, sighing deeply.*)

(**BERT** *has turned toward the corner.*)

Bertram?

(**BERT** *turns to her.*)

Bertram, I love you, do you hear me?

(**BERT** *slowly crosses downstage toward the entrance to the basement, stops just before the threshold. They lock eyes during cross, beholding each other in a gaze of gentle terror.*)

Did you hear me, Bertram?

(**CORA** *turns to* **JAMES**.)

(**CELESTE** *turns to the she-lion.*)

(**WILMA** *enters, starts to clear the table. While clearing, she sings the following song:**)

WILMA.

   I CAN SEE YOU
   I CAN SEE THE ANIMALS TOO

---

*A license to produce *Dreams of Flying Dreams of Falling* does not include a performance license for any third-party or copyrighted melodies. Licensees should create their own.

I CAN SEE THAT PLACE INSIDE
WHERE THE FAIRIES OF THE FOREST HIDE
I AM FLYING
WILL YOU FLY WITH ME?
O'ER VOLCANOES,
SILVER WATERFALLS
AND THE DEEPEST, VELVET SEA

I AM FALLING
WILL YOU FALL WITH ME?
WE'LL FALL SO GENTLY
THROUGH THE NIGHT
LIKE POLLEN
AND BLACK APPLES
FORGOTTEN SPARROWS
TAKING FLIGHT

I AM DREAMING
WILL YOU DREAM WITH ME?
WE ARE DREAMING
THAT WE'RE FLYING
AND FALLING
AND FLYING
AND FALLING
FALLING...

> (**BERT** *and* **SANDRA** *continue to lock eyes.*)
>
> (**WILMA** *continues clearing and singing, wiping down the table.*)
>
> (*The others freeze as lights fade to black.*)

End of Play